WHOSE MANGEF

LISA ROBBINS

Illustrated by

TATIANA KOCHAN

A Christian Company
ElkLakePublishingInc.com

Cover and Interior Design: Tatiana Kochan, Derinda Babcock
Editor(s): Donna Wyland, Derinda Babcock, Deb Haggerty

PUBLISHED BY: Elk Lake Publishing, Inc., 35 Dogwood Drive, Plymouth, MA 02360, 2023

Library Cataloging Data

Names: Robbins, Lisa (Lisa Robbins)

Whose Manger is This? / Lisa Robbins

32 p. 21.6 cm × 21.6 cm (8.5 in × 8.5 in.)

ISBN-13: 9798891340558 (paperback) | 9798891340565 (trade hardcover) | 9798891340572 (trade paperback) | 9798891340589 (e-book)

Key Words: Christmas Holiday; Animals; God's Son Jesus King; Manger; Give Gifts; Worship Praise; Joy

"Why is a baby in the manger where we eat?"
asked Rowdy Old Ram as he stomped his four feet.

"This is my manger," Rowdy Ram said to Cow.

"Go away. I am hungry. I want my food now."

"This is my manger," Cranky Cow said to Mule.

"Go away from my stable. In this place I rule."

"This is my manger," Moody Mule said to Camel.

"Go away. I must eat, you tall fuzzy mammal."

"This is my manger," Curt Camel said to Jay.

"Go away or I'll spit, go away, go away."

"This is my manger," Jeering Jay said to Dove.

"Go away. I must peck for the food that I love."

"This is my manger," Dapper Dove said to Mouse.

"Go away. I want hay to build my new house."

"This is my manger," Meanie Mouse said to Cat.

"Go away. I need hay for my nest, now you scat."

"This is my manger," Cozy Cat said to Ram.

"Go away while I curl up to sleep—now scram."

18

"You cannot sleep there," Rowdy Ram had his say.
"The baby is still sound asleep on the hay."

19

The animals looked at the baby wrapped tight.
God's Son, heaven's gift, had been born in the night.

They moved near the manger, then gathered around.
The animals stood still. Not one made a sound.

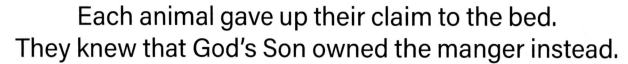
Each animal gave up their claim to the bed.
They knew that God's Son owned the manger instead.

24

With joy in their hearts, they started to sing.
Then the animals each brought their gifts to the King.

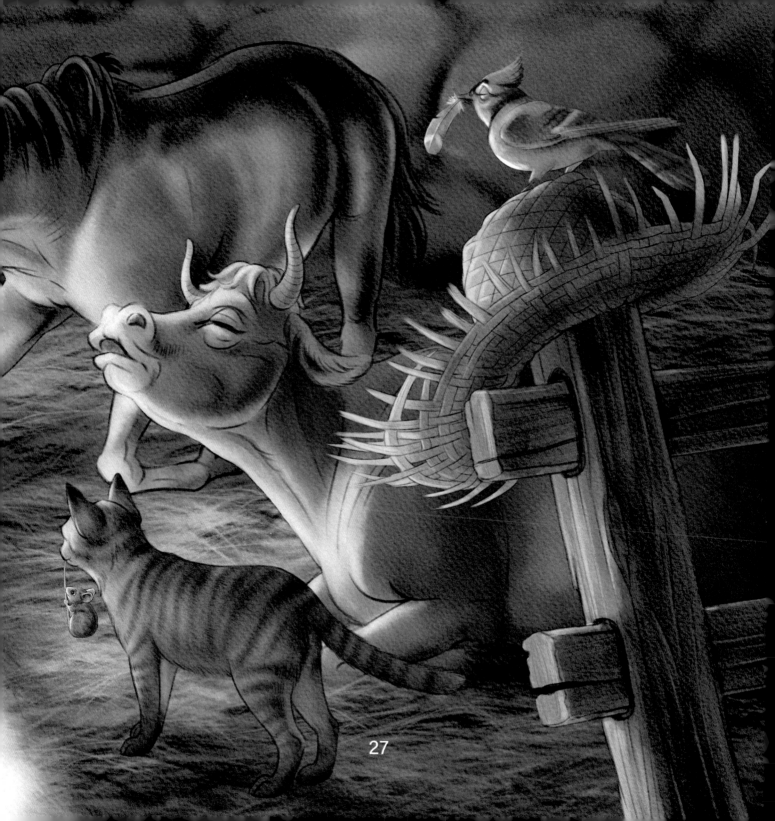

27

ABOUT THE AUTHOR

Lisa Robbins is a wife, mom, and nana who lives in rural Tennessee. Teaching children God's truth in a creative and fun way is a passion she has pursued for many years. Lisa's lively lessons are filled with spirited expression, large visuals, and energetic role play. Believing God's Word has the power to change lives, especially little lives, compels Lisa to fulfill her Kingdom purpose of teaching and writing. When she's not pursuing those activities, Lisa attends church, participates in community ministry, spends time with her family, and plays with her grandchildren. She also enjoys reading, traveling, and thrifting. Visit Lisa at: www.lisarobbinsauthor.com

Let's Talk About Behaving

Rowdy Ram roughly stomps his feet.
What might be a better way to react when you're not happy about something?

Cranky Cow gets upset while wanting to rule.
What is a better way to let others know you are upset?

Moody Mule throws a fit.
How could you use your words to let someone know you don't like what is happening?

Curt Camel demands his want above the needs of others.
What are some ways you can show others that you're willing to share?

Jeering Jay yells loudly.
Describe a time you used your quiet voice to ask for something you want.

Dapper Dove struggles to be still.
What helps you be still?

Meanie Mouse is mean and tricky.
List some ways you can be kind and honest with others.

Cozy Cat only cares about being comfortable.
How can you help others feel comfortable?

The joyful animals praised Jesus with song and gave him gifts.
We can all give Jesus the gift of praise with our voices!
What else might we give Jesus?

Who Gave the Gift?

Look at the gifts in the picture and name each animal that gave that gift.

red scarf
star bell
straw hat
red blanket
feather
mouse
herself

Once the animals give up their bad behaviors,
they see baby Jesus and bow to worship.
What are other ways to worship Jesus?

Made in the USA
Middletown, DE
16 October 2023